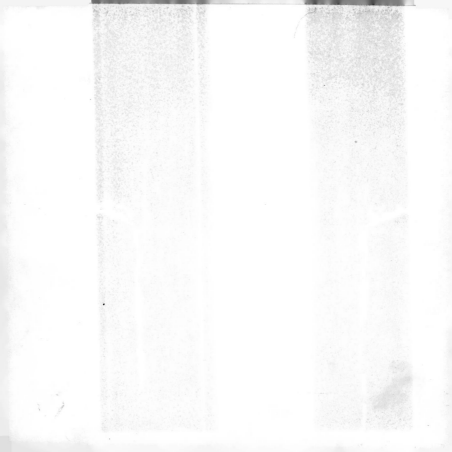

MR. BUSY™

by Roger Hargreaves

20 19 18 17 16 15 14 13 12 11 10

PRICE STERN SLOAN
Los Angeles

There has never been anybody quite like Mr. Busy.

He could do things ten times as fast as you or I could.

For instance, if he was reading this book, he'd have finished it by now.

He lived in a very busy-looking house which he'd built himself.

As you can see.

It had lots of doors and windows, and do you know what it was called?

Weekend Cottage!

Do you know why?

Because that's how long it took him to build it!

One fine summer morning Mr. Busy was up bright and early at 6 o'clock.

He jumped out of bed and took a bath and brushed his teeth and cooked his breakfast and ate his breakfast and read the paper and washed up and made his bed and cleaned the house from top to bottom.

By that time it was 7 o'clock.

Busy Mr. Busy!

Now, next door to Mr. Busy lived someone
who wasn't quite such a busy person.

In fact, a very unbusy person.

Mr. Slow!

If he was reading this book, he'd . . . read . . . it . . . like . . . this!

He'd still be on the first page!

And that same fine summer morning, at five after seven, when Mr. Busy knocked at his door Mr. Slow was fast asleep in bed.

He'd gone to bed for an afternoon nap the day before and somehow hadn't awakened until he heard Mr. Busy knocking at his door.

"Who's . . . that . . . knocking . . . at . . . my . . . door?" he called downstairs.

"Good morning," cried Mr. Busy. "Can I come in?"

And, without waiting for an answer, he went inside.

"Where are you?" he called.

"Up . . . stairs," came the slow reply.

So Mr. Busy went up the steps, two at a time.

"Good heavens," he said. "You're still in bed!"

And he made Mr. Slow get up.

And he made his bed for him, and cooked his breakfast for him, and cleaned his house for him.

Poor Mr. Slow.

He hated to be rushed and fussed over.

"Okay," said Mr. Busy briskly. "It's a fine day. Let's go on a picnic."

Mr. Slow made a face.

"I . . . don't . . . like . . . picnics," he complained.

"Nonsense," replied Mr. Busy and busied himself in Mr. Slow's kitchen making a picnic lunch for the two of them.

It took him a minute and a half.

"Okay," he cried, when he'd finished. "Off we go!"

And he hurried Mr. Slow out his front door and off they went.

As you can imagine Mr. Busy walks extremely quickly.

And, as you can imagine, Mr. Slow doesn't.

So, by the time Mr. Busy had walked a mile do you know how far Mr. Slow had walked?

To his own garden gate!

Mr. Busy hurried back.

"Come on," he cried impatiently. "Hurry up!"

"Hurry . . . up," replied Mr. Slow.

"Im . . . poss . . . i . . . ble!"

"Oh, all right," said Mr. Busy. "We'll have a picnic in your garden."

"Wait a minute though," he added. "The grass needs cutting."

And he rushed back to Weekend Cottage and rushed back again with his lawnmower and rushed up and down cutting Mr. Slow's lawn.

It took him two and a half minutes!

It would have taken him two minutes but he had to mow around Mr. Slow who couldn't get out of the way in time.

"Okay," cried Mr. Busy. "Picnic time!"

And together on that fine summer day they had a fine picnic.

Well, actually, Mr. Busy had a finer picnic than Mr. Slow because he ate more quickly and had most of the food.

Mr. Busy stretched out on the grass.

"That was fun," he said. "I like picnics!"

"You . . . do! . . . I . . . don't," said Mr. Slow.

"Tell you what," went on Mr. Busy, ignoring him. "Tomorrow we'll go on a real picnic, out in the country."

Mr. Slow made a face.

"And," went on Mr. Busy, "in order to do that and get you out into the country I'll have to call for you earlier than I did this morning."

Mr. Slow made another face.

"See you tomorrow then," said Mr. Busy, and went home and cleaned his house from bottom to top.

The following morning Mr. Busy jumped out of bed at 5 o'clock and took a bath and brushed his teeth and cooked his breakfast and ate his breakfast and read the paper and washed up and made his bed and cleaned the house from top to bottom.

By that time it was 6 o'clock.

He went and knocked on Mr. Slow's front door.

"Come on! Come on!" he cried. "Time to be up and about! Picnic day!"

Under his bed Mr. Slow smiled a slow smile.

And he wasn't anywhere upstairs.

And he wasn't anywhere downstairs.

"Drat," said Mr. Busy. "I wonder where he's gone."

Where Mr. Slow had gone was under his bed.

To hide!

He didn't want to go on any picnic.

Not he.

"Drat," said Mr. Busy again. "That means I'll have to go on a picnic by myself."

No reply.

"Come on," cried Mr. Busy again.

No reply.

Mr. Busy went inside.

And went up the steps, three at a time, and into Mr. Slow's bedroom expecting to find him in bed.

But he wasn't.